This book belongs to

....

For Dave, and Roxy dog

Goose Goes to the Zoo
Copyright © 2016 by Laura Wall
All rights reserved. Manufactured in China.

www.harpercollinschildrens.com

ISBN 978-0-06-232441-2 (trade bdg.)

The artwork for this book was drawn with charcoal and finished digitally.

15 16 17 18 19 SCP 10 9 8 7 6 5 4 3 2 1

First U.S. edition, 2016

Originally published in the U.K. in 2012 by Award Publications Limited

Goose
GOES TO THE ZOO

by Laura Wall

HARPER

An Imprint of HarperCollinsPublishers

Sophie and Goose are best friends.

They do everything together.

But there are some things that
Sophie and Goose can't do together.

Sophie can't fly.

She's not fond of goose food, either.

And when Sophie goes to school,
Goose has to stay home.

Sophie worries that Goose is
lonely when she is at school.

Perhaps Goose needs another
friend to play with, too?

Sophie wonders where she
can find a friend for Goose.

Then she has a marvelous idea. The zoo!

There are all sorts of strange noises
coming from inside the zoo.

But Goose isn't scared.

So together they go through the gates . . .

. . . and into the zoo.

Sophie finds a big spotty giraffe.

He seems nice and friendly, but he can't fly.

No matter how hard they try.

Goose sees a smiling crocodile in the pool.

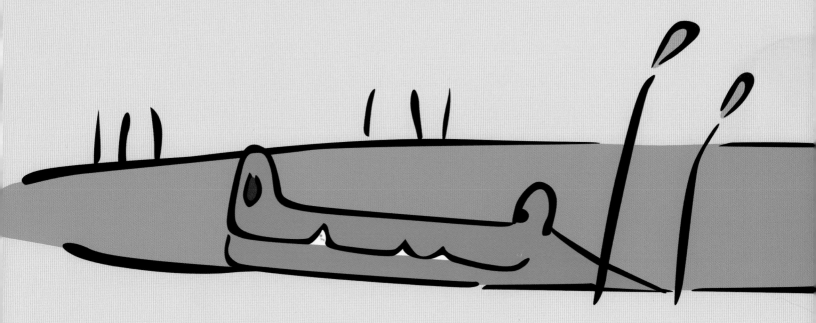

Perhaps he could be Goose's new friend.

But he likes the wrong kind of goose food!

Sophie and Goose find some pink birds.

But they don't seem to do much!

Oh dear. Poor Goose.

Then Sophie and Goose
hear a familiar sound.

Honk!
honk!

honk
Honk!

honk
Honk!

Honk!
honk!
honk

honk

honk
Honk!

honk

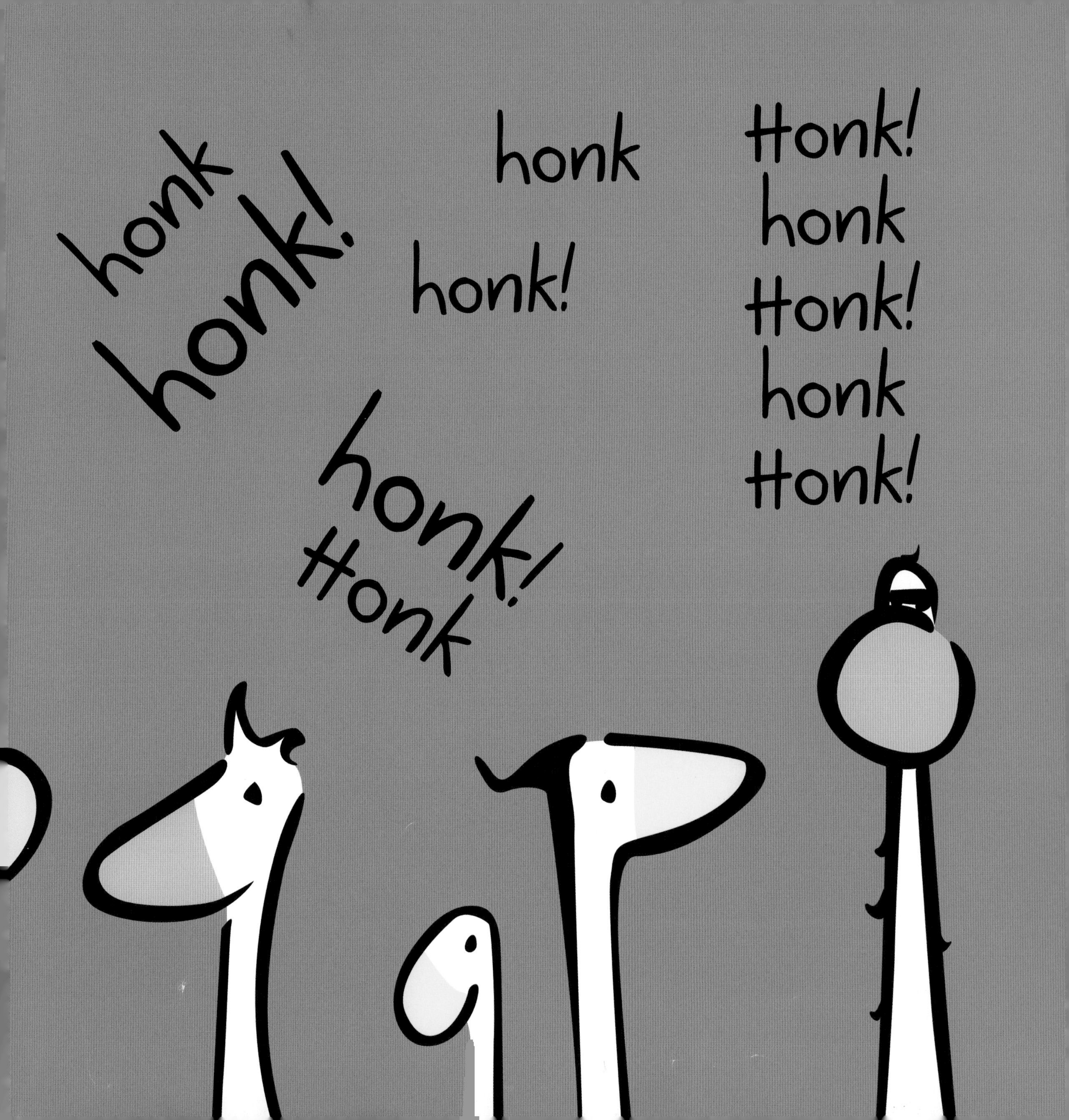
honk
honk!
honk
honk!
honk!
Honk
Honk!
honk
Honk!
honk
Honk!

"Look! Lots of geese, just like you!"

They ask Goose to fly with them.

And they share a snack.

They seem like very good company.

Sophie's glad Goose has found some new friends to play with.

She is happy for Goose.

Really, she is.

And Goose likes his new friends, too.

But there's no friend quite like Sophie.